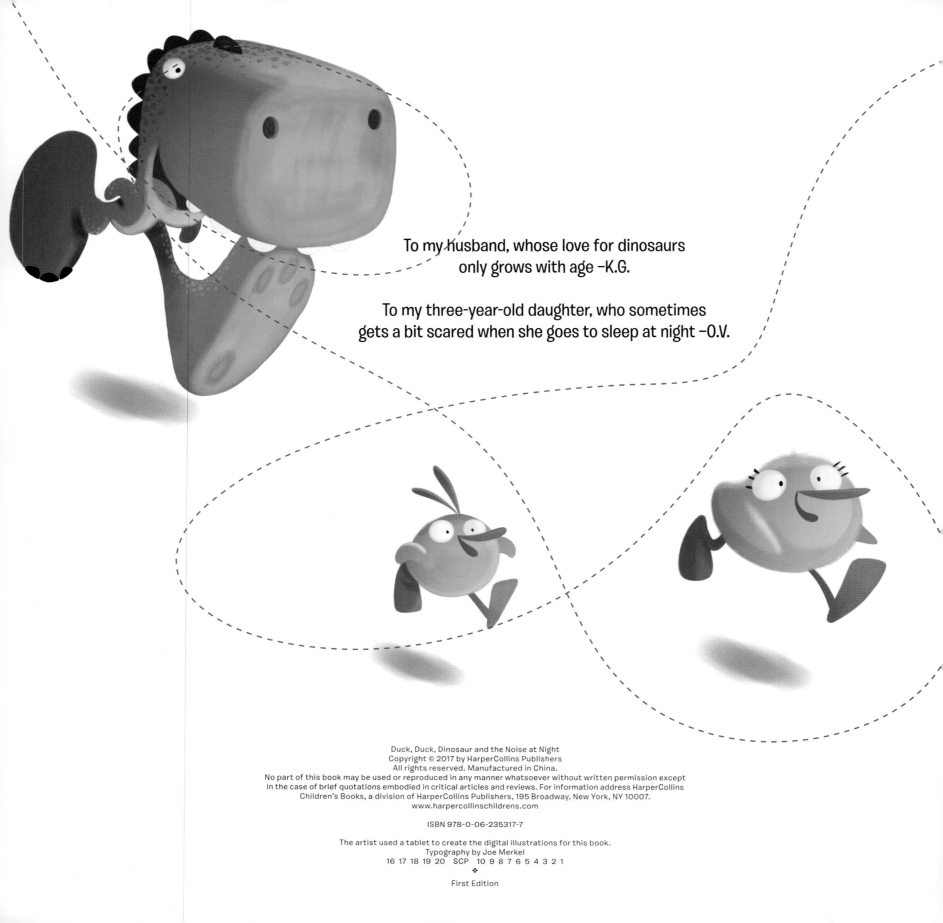

To my husband, whose love for dinosaurs
only grows with age –K.G.

To my three-year-old daughter, who sometimes
gets a bit scared when she goes to sleep at night –O.V.

Duck, Duck, Dinosaur and the Noise at Night
Copyright © 2017 by HarperCollins Publishers
All rights reserved. Manufactured in China.
No part of this book may be used or reproduced in any manner whatsoever without written permission except
in the case of brief quotations embodied in critical articles and reviews. For information address HarperCollins
Children's Books, a division of HarperCollins Publishers, 195 Broadway, New York, NY 10007.
www.harpercollinschildrens.com

ISBN 978-0-06-235317-7

The artist used a tablet to create the digital illustrations for this book.
Typography by Joe Merkel
16 17 18 19 20   SCP   10 9 8 7 6 5 4 3 2 1
❖
First Edition

DUCK, DUCK, DINOSAUR

AND THE
NOISE AT NIGHT

Kallie George • Illustrated by Oriol Vidal

HARPER

An Imprint of HarperCollinsPublishers

Mama Duck's family was growing up fast.

Flap was getting big.

Feather was getting big.

And Spike was getting . . . bigger!

They were too big to sleep with Mama Duck.
It was time for them to sleep all by themselves
in their very own nest.

They were excited and only a little scared.
"We are ready!" said Feather. "We can do it!"

Feather, Flap, and Spike shared a story.

They shared a snuggle.

Then they fell asleep.

They all woke up at once.

"I heard a noise! A scary noise!" said Flap.

"I heard it, too," said Feather. "But what can we
do? We can't just hide. . . ."

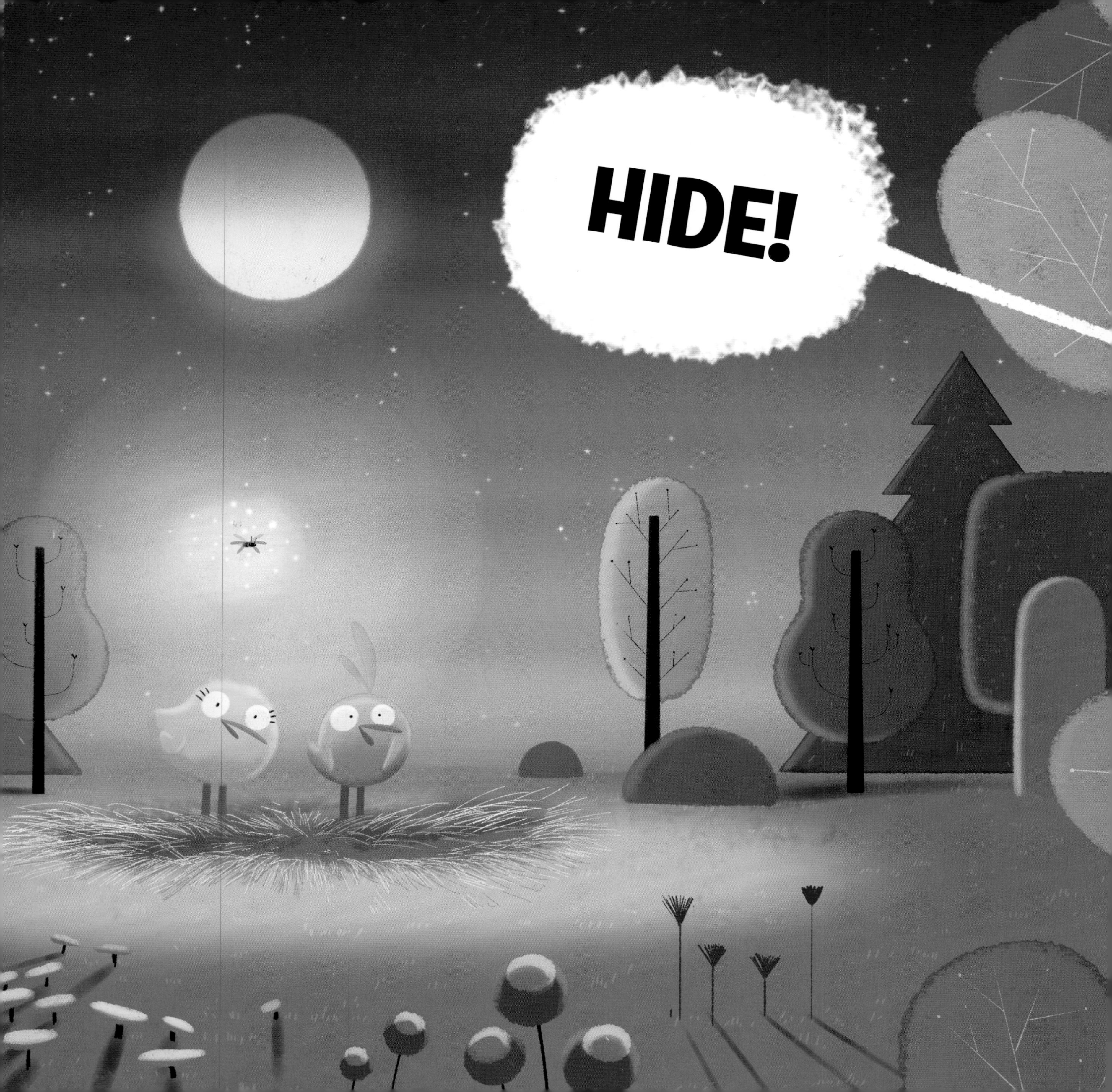
HIDE!

Spike hid.

So Feather and Flap hid, too.

They shared a story.

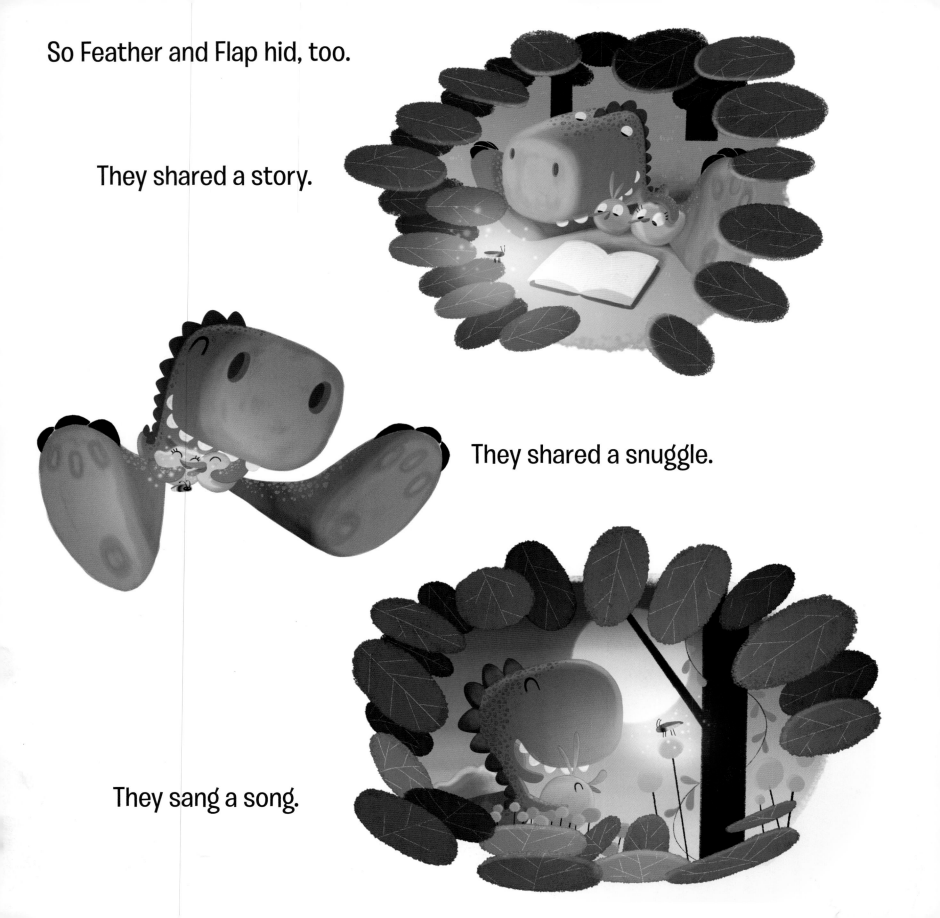

They shared a snuggle.

They sang a song.

Then, at last, they fell asleep.

GRRORE!

They all woke up at once.

"I heard that noise!
That scary noise!" said Flap.

"I heard it, too," said Feather. "Hiding didn't work.
But what else can we do? We can't just run away. . . ."

Spike ran away. So Feather and Flap ran away, too.
They ran and ran, all the way around the pond.

They were too tired to take another step.

They shared a story. They shared a snuggle.
They sang a song. They counted the stars.

Then, at last, they fell asleep.

GRRORE!

They all woke up at once.

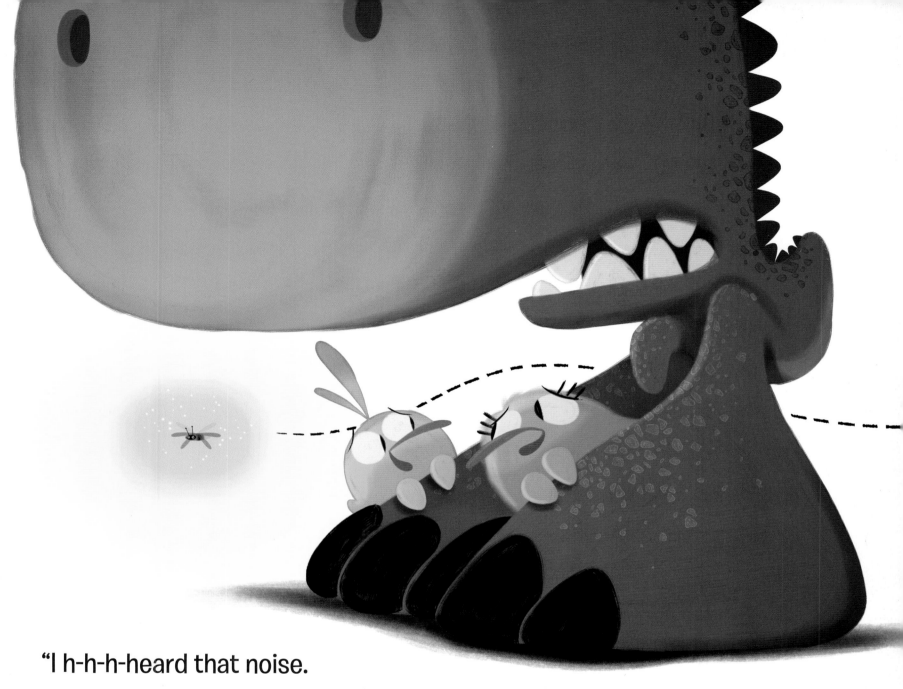

"I h-h-h-heard that noise.
That s-s-s-scary noise," said Flap.

"I heard it, too." Feather trembled. "Hiding didn't work.
Running away didn't work. There's nothing we can do!"

It was late and they were scared.
Feather's knees knocked.
Flap's wings flapped.
And Spike's teeth chattered.

CHATTER

CHATTER!

CHATTER

Everyone was being so . . .

"That's it! We can be *really* noisy!" said
Feather. "We can scare the scary noise."

Feather and Flap made all kinds of noises.

But Spike made only one . . .

GRRRORE!

The GRRORE was a SNORE!
It was Spike.

Flap laughed. Feather laughed.
They would tell Spike in the morning.

Feather and Flap didn't share a story or a snuggle or sing a song or count the stars. They didn't need to. They fell straight to sleep.

And they slept in their very own nest
all night long.